The Christmas Heist

A Heartwarming Christmas Mystery Novel in the Tradition of Large Print Fiction Books

Ivy J Frost

Chapter 1

The snow had been falling steadily since morning, turning the world outside into a picture-perfect postcard. The lawns of Evergreen Retirement Home were blanketed in thick, glistening white. Icicles clung to the gutters, and the soft glow of the Christmas lights lit up the windows like warm beacons against the cold.

Inside the common room, the residents of Evergreen sat in their usual spots, bundled in layers of wool and fleece, each holding a bingo card. The fire crackled in the hearth, sending occasional pops through the room. The smell of cinnamon cookies and peppermint tea lingered in the air.

"B-7," called Margaret, the young activities director with an eternally cheerful voice. "That's B... seven."

"Got it!" Dot O'Hara whispered to herself. She dabbed her marker on the card in her lap with a soft thunk. Dot was the kind of person who wore cardigans year-round and still kept tissues tucked up her sleeve. She smiled even when no one was watching, and her thin, silver hair curled around her ears like a halo.

Edna Bishop, sitting to Dot's right, leaned over with a smirk. "Three in a row already?"

Dot blushed. "Well, I do like my numbers."

"You like something, all right," muttered Frank Holloway from across the table. He was slouched in his chair, arms crossed over a thick green sweater with a snowman on it—ironically worn, of course. Frank had a voice like gravel and a permanent scowl that made most of the staff nervous. But under that bark was a good man with a soft spot for stray cats and crossword puzzles.

"Don't be jealous just 'cause Dot's winning," Edna said with a wink. "Maybe if you smiled once in a while, the Bingo Gods would show you mercy."

Frank rolled his eyes. "I smiled in '68. Didn't like it."

Edna let out a delighted cackle. At seventy-eight, she was the unofficial queen of Evergreen. Bold lipstick, sensible shoes, and a mouth that had never learned to stay shut. Her hair was always done, and her opinions were even more styled.

Across from her, Harold Finch adjusted his bifocals and carefully dabbed his own card. He was quiet, bookish, and always seemed to be reading something—today it was a crime novel with a snow-covered mansion on the cover. Once a school librarian, Harold rarely raised his voice but always had a sharp comment when it counted.

"N-42," Margaret called.

"Bingo!" cried Dot.

Edna clapped. "There she goes again, the Snow Angel of Evergreen."

Margaret walked over to check the card. "We have a winner!" she said brightly. "Dot, would you like the peppermint candle or the mystery box?"

Dot bit her lip. "Oh... mystery, I think."

"Living dangerously," Edna teased.

As Margaret handed over the prize—a lumpy, tissue-wrapped package—Edna leaned back in her chair and sighed contentedly. She loved this time of year. Even here, in a building full of aching joints and early bedtimes, Christmas still brought a little magic. The tree in the corner sparkled, the music hummed softly in the background, and the world seemed, for just a moment, almost right.

But then, she heard something.

Two staff members were standing just outside the door to the common room, whispering in low voices. They probably thought the bingo crowd wasn't paying attention—but Edna had good ears when she wanted to. She turned slightly, pretending to stretch her neck, and listened.

"...they're not going to notice," said the first voice. Male. Young. Probably the night security guy, Tyler.

"It's the town's Christmas fund," the second voice replied—a woman. Sounded like Janet, the administrative assistant. "It's supposed to go to the food bank and the kids' coats drive."

There was a pause.

"Look," Tyler said. "Mr. Grafton said he'd 'handle' it. Who's going to argue with the treasurer? Anyway, it's just sitting there. Unclaimed donations, he called it."

Unclaimed?

Edna's ears perked up.

Janet's voice lowered further. "It just feels wrong. That's all."

Edna straightened up and looked over at Harold, who had also paused mid-dab. Their eyes met. He'd heard it too.

Frank grunted. "You're frowning."

Edna didn't answer.

Instead, she stood and walked toward the snack table under the guise of refilling her tea. Dot followed, cradling her mystery box.

"You okay, Edna?" Dot asked sweetly.

"I just heard something," Edna said, keeping her voice low. "Something about the town's Christmas fund."

Dot frowned. "The donation fund? The one with all the coats and meals for the needy?"

Edna nodded slowly. "Apparently, our upstanding town treasurer is 'handling' it. Doesn't sound like he's handling it very nicely."

Harold appeared beside them, quietly pouring himself some cider.

"I heard it too," he said. "Sounds like someone's been dipping into the donation pot."

Dot gasped. "That's awful!"

Edna narrowed her eyes toward the hallway where the voices had faded.

"Do you know how much money gets raised for that fund each year?" Edna muttered. "The town's Christmas auction alone pulls in thousands. Not to mention the charity gala."

Harold adjusted his glasses. "If Grafton's skimming, no one would notice until January. By then, the holidays are over and the food banks are empty."

Frank had wandered over now, frowning.

"Don't tell me you're getting riled up over gossip," he said. "Let the authorities deal with it."

"Authorities?" Edna scoffed. "You mean the ones who think we're all half-asleep in our pudding?"

Frank crossed his arms again. "You planning to do something about it?"

Edna paused. Her lips curled into a sly smile.

"Maybe I am," she said. "Maybe it's time someone did."

. . .

Later that evening, after the bingo cards were packed away and most of the residents had drifted off to their rooms, Edna sat by the big window in the lounge, watching the snow fall.

The Christmas lights twinkled across the courtyard. Somewhere, someone was playing carols on a piano, off-key but full of heart. Edna held her cup of tea close to her chest and thought.

She'd lived a long life. Raised three kids, buried one husband, traveled a bit, retired quietly. But somewhere along the way, the world had started looking past her—like she was furniture. Comfortable, familiar... and easy to ignore.

But she wasn't done yet.

Not if there were kids going cold and hungry because some slick-haired town treasurer thought no one would notice.

Harold sat down next to her with a book tucked under his arm.

"You really mean it, don't you?" he said. "You want to do something."

Edna turned to him. "Why not?"

"We're old."

Edna snorted. "So?"

Harold looked thoughtful. "You're going to need a plan."

"I always have a plan."

At that moment, Dot padded in with her slippers whispering against the tile. She was holding a tray with cocoa for everyone.

"I brought marshmallows," she whispered.

"Dot," Edna said, "how would you feel about righting a wrong?"

Dot blinked. "Oh. Well, that depends. Is there sneaking involved?"

"Possibly."

She smiled. "Then I'm in."

Frank showed up next, leaning on his cane.

"I can't believe I'm saying this," he muttered, "but if you're going to stick your noses where they don't belong, someone's got to be around to keep you alive."

Edna raised her cup in salute. "Welcome to the resistance, boys and girls."

Harold chuckled softly. "We'll need information. Evidence. Something to prove what he's doing."

Edna nodded. "And we'll need to get into that office of his before he moves the money somewhere else."

Frank sighed. "This is a stupid idea."

"But?" Edna prompted.

"But I haven't been this interested in something in ten years."

Dot giggled. "It's like one of those mystery books you read, Harold."

"No," Harold said, smiling faintly. "This is better. Because in this one… we're the main characters."

Outside the window, snow kept falling, wrapping the town in soft silence. But inside Evergreen, something new was stirring. Not just mischief. Not just a heist.

Something warmer. Sharper.

The Christmas Heist

Hope.

Edna sat up straighter.

"Someone ought to do something about it," she whispered again.

And now... someone would.

Chapter 2

The next night, the common room at Evergreen Retirement Home looked like it always did after dinner — quiet, cozy, and dimly lit with soft amber lamps. But something was different. Something was... brewing.

Edna Bishop checked her watch — 7:05 p.m.

"Fashionably late," she muttered.

She sat at a small round table in the far corner, tucked beside a tall bookshelf that blocked most of the room from view. A stack of old magazines and a dried-out poinsettia acted as a kind of camouflage. From a distance, it looked like nothing more than a spot for reading or a snooze. But up close, it was headquarters.

The first to arrive was Harold Finch. He shuffled in carrying his crime novel and a thermos of chamomile tea. He sat across from Edna, pushed his glasses up his nose, and gave a single nod. No words needed. He was in.

Dot O'Hara followed a minute later, clutching a tote bag with an embroidered snowman on it. She looked around nervously and lowered her voice.

"Should I have brought cookies? I brought my notebook. And some licorice."

"We're not baking a pie, Dot," Edna said with a smile. "We're planning a heist."

"Oh, right."

The last to appear was Frank Holloway. He stomped in with his cane, muttering something about "damn cold tiles," and sat down heavily.

"You all realize how ridiculous this is?" he grumbled.

Edna leaned forward. "Not ridiculous. Necessary."

Frank sighed and looked around the table. "So what's the plan? We storm Town Hall, demand the donation fund, and hold the treasurer hostage with a plate of gingerbread men?"

"Not quite," Edna said. "We need to be smart. Precise. Invisible."

"Invisible?" Dot asked. "We're all over seventy, Edna."

"Exactly," she replied, tapping her temple. "No one expects people like us to do anything daring. That's our power. We're not invisible because we're weak — we're invisible because people stopped looking. That's their mistake."

Harold leaned back slightly. "And we're going to use that to our advantage."

Frank narrowed his eyes. "Have any of you actually broken into a building before?"

Edna lifted her chin. "I once snuck into the principal's office in 1962 to get my son out of detention. Does that count?"

The Christmas Heist

Frank didn't look impressed.

"Look," Edna said, "we're not robbing a bank. We're taking back money that was meant for kids. Warm coats. Christmas meals. If Grafton's keeping it for himself, then we're just... giving it back to the people it belongs to."

Dot perked up. "Like Robin Hood!"

"Exactly," Edna said. "Only with more fiber supplements."

Frank let out a reluctant chuckle.

Harold opened a small notebook of his own and flipped through a few pages.

"I did a little research," he said. "Grafton's office is in the back of Town Hall. The donation fund is stored in a wall safe behind his desk — I saw it when I visited to renew my ID last spring."

Dot gasped. "You've been in there? What's it like?"

"Boring. Too much beige. But the safe is a small one, probably a four-digit combination.

Nothing a real criminal couldn't crack in five minutes."

Frank raised an eyebrow. "And what makes you think we can crack it?"

Harold adjusted his glasses. "Because I used to be a locksmith. In college. Worked weekends. I still remember the basics. I can pick a simple lock, and I've been practicing on the filing cabinet in my room."

Dot clapped her hands. "That's amazing, Harold!"

He blushed. "It's not much. But it might be enough."

Edna looked over at Dot. "What about you? Got any secret talents?"

Dot fidgeted with the strap of her tote bag. "Well... I do have these." She tapped her ears gently. "My hearing aids. The new ones I got last month? They're digital. They can record sound."

"Seriously?" Frank asked.

Dot nodded. "My nephew set it up for me. All I have to do is tap this button on the side and it records everything I hear."

Harold looked impressed. "That could be useful. We'll need proof. Something that shows what Grafton's up to before we make our move."

Edna gave Dot an approving smile. "See? Every elf in Santa's workshop has a purpose."

Frank grunted. "And what am I? The reindeer?"

"You," Edna said, pointing a finger at him, "still have your driver's license. You're the only one here who can drive after dark and not confuse a stop sign for a mailbox."

Frank frowned. "I haven't driven at night in months."

"But you *can*," she pressed.

He sighed. "Yes, I can."

"Then you're the getaway sleigh."

Dot giggled again. "We're like the Santa Squad!"

Everyone turned to her.

"What?" she said. "It just popped into my head."

Edna smiled. "No, it's perfect."

Harold nodded slowly. "The Santa Squad. I like it."

Frank grumbled something under his breath but didn't argue.

Edna leaned forward, her eyes glinting. "Alright then. Here's what we do: we gather evidence first. Dot, you keep your ears open. If we can get Grafton admitting anything on tape, that's our golden ticket. Harold, see if you can sketch the office layout from memory. We'll need to know what kind of safe we're dealing with."

"And me?" Frank asked.

"You," Edna said, "are going to check if your car still runs. And maybe take it around the block to see if it can do more than fifteen miles an hour."

Frank looked offended. "It can do *twenty*."

Dot raised her hand. "Um... should we wear disguises?"

Harold tilted his head. "We already look like everyone's great-aunt or grandfather."

"Still," Edna said thoughtfully. "Maybe some festive flair. Santa hats. Scarves. Ugly sweaters. The town will be crawling with carolers on Christmas Eve. If we time it right, we'll blend right in."

"Wait a second," Frank said. "You're thinking of doing this *on Christmas Eve?*"

"Of course," Edna replied. "Town Hall is closed. Grafton will be at the Mayor's Gala. The streets will be quiet. Everyone will be focused on turkey and tinsel. It's the perfect time."

"Perfect for getting arrested," Frank muttered.

"But perfect," Harold said.

There was a moment of silence as the four of them sat there, surrounded by the hum of the heater and the distant jingle of a Christmas playlist on someone's radio.

Edna looked around the table at her unlikely team. A quiet librarian. A cardigan-loving sweetheart. A grumpy vet. And herself — a retired teacher with too much time and not enough patience for corruption.

"I don't know about you," she said softly, "but I don't want to sit in this chair for the rest of my life, watching the world go wrong and doing nothing about it. We may be old… but we still matter. And if this is how we go out, then by God, let it be in a blaze of Christmas glory."

Dot wiped a tear from her eye.

Harold smiled faintly.

Frank scratched his beard. "We're all insane."

Edna raised her cup.

"To the Santa Squad."

The others joined her, their mugs clinking softly in the candlelight.

"To justice," said Harold.

"To helping people," whispered Dot.

"To not crashing the car," grumbled Frank.

The Christmas Heist

The snow began to fall again outside, soft and slow. And in that quiet lounge at Evergreen Retirement Home, a plan began to take shape — bold, ridiculous, and entirely heartwarming.

Operation Christmas Heist was on its way.

Chapter 3

Two days later, the Santa Squad gathered again.

The meeting place hadn't changed: the quiet corner of the common room, hidden behind a tall bookshelf that still displayed a stack of magazines no one had touched since Easter. Dot brought scones this time, wrapped in a Christmas napkin. Frank brought nothing but complaints. Harold brought a blueprint he had sketched on three pages of printer paper taped together.

"Town Hall," he said, laying it out gently across the table. "It's not exactly Fort Knox."

Edna leaned in, eyebrows raised. "Let's see it."

Harold tapped his pen against the first section. "Front entrance here. They close it by five o'clock every day. Security is light — just one camera over the door, probably old. No guard, just Tyler doing random rounds."

"The same Tyler who barely stays awake on bingo nights?" Edna asked.

Harold nodded. "Exactly. The doors stay locked after hours, but there's a key box in the alley. Custodians use it."

Dot gasped. "You know the code?"

Harold gave a sly smile. "No. But I know how to find out."

Edna grinned. "I'm starting to like this side of you, Harold."

Harold moved his finger to the center of the paper. "Now, the treasurer's office. Back hallway, second floor, farthest room. Corner office. Big oak door. And here—" he tapped again, "—is where I saw the safe. Behind a fake painting of a sailing ship."

Dot leaned over the blueprint, frowning. "How big is the safe?"

"Not huge. About the size of a microwave."

Frank finally spoke. "And what makes you think there's money in there?"

Harold sat back. "Because I went back today."

"You what?" Edna said, blinking.

"I told the clerk I'd lost my wallet at my last visit and asked to check the lobby. While I was there, I saw Grafton through the door. The office was open. He had the safe open. He was counting cash. Big stacks of it."

Dot's eyes went wide. "Stacks?"

Frank snorted. "Could've been Monopoly money."

"Nope," Harold said. "Real bills. Neatly rubber-banded. And the envelope he dropped one stack into had a label. Said: *Holiday Relief Fund.*"

There was silence at the table. The fire in the hearth crackled in the distance.

Edna clenched her teacup. "He's hoarding it."

Dot looked distressed. "But that's meant for families. For people who don't have coats. Kids who won't get toys this year."

Edna sat back, fire in her eyes. "He's sitting on it like a dragon guarding treasure."

Harold nodded slowly. "Probably intends to move it after the holidays. Maybe pocket some, or call it a 'budget overage' and move it into some made-up expense."

"And no one's the wiser," Frank added bitterly.

"Unless," Edna said, "someone stops him."

Dot fidgeted. "Do we know where he'll be Christmas Eve?"

"Oh yes," Edna said. "The Mayor's Gala. Annual thing at the community center. He's always there. In a suit that looks like it hasn't fit him since the '90s. I checked the event flyer posted near the mailboxes."

"And what time does it start?" Harold asked.

"Seven o'clock sharp. Dinner. Dancing. Half the town will be there."

Frank raised an eyebrow. "So while Grafton's doing the foxtrot, we're breaking into Town Hall?"

"That's the idea."

Dot raised her hand. "Won't the building be alarmed?"

Harold answered. "Old system. I saw the panel. One of those keypads from the '90s. The code is probably something dumb like 1-2-3-4."

"We're not guessing codes," Frank growled.

"We won't have to," Harold said. "I can loop the entry system if I access the panel within 30 seconds of entering. I've been brushing up."

Edna chuckled. "What have you been brushing up with, Harold?"

He shrugged. "Internet. Dot's nephew helped me download a few videos."

Dot smiled proudly. "He's very good with technology. Has his own drone!"

Frank rolled his eyes. "Great. We'll steal Christmas using YouTube tutorials."

The Christmas Heist

Edna pressed her hands together. "Let's focus. Harold's our key man. Frank, you'll drive us. Dot, you're lookout and communications. Your hearing aids can pick up chatter, and we'll rig you a radio."

Dot blinked. "A radio?"

Harold smiled. "Easy. I have walkie-talkies in my closet. My nephew gave them to me last Christmas. Thought I could use them during fire drills. We'll test them tomorrow."

Edna nodded. "Perfect. I'll go in with Harold. I'll handle lookout inside and help carry the loot — that is, the rightful donations."

Frank leaned back in his chair, hands crossed. "You all realize we're probably committing at least four crimes."

"Yes," Edna said brightly. "But it's Christmas."

Frank stared at her. "That's your defense?"

"Tell me something, Frank," she said. "You served in the military, right?"

"Yes."

"Ever bend the rules to protect someone who couldn't protect themselves?"

He didn't answer right away. Then he grunted. "Plenty of times."

"Well," Edna said, "this is one of those times. Except instead of camouflage and field radios, we've got scarves and arthritis pills."

Dot giggled. Harold smiled.

Frank sighed. "I must've hit my head this morning."

"You're in, then?" Edna asked.

He looked around at their expectant faces, the crooked little blueprint on the table, the flicker of hope in Dot's eyes.

"...Yeah," he muttered. "I'm in."

Edna sat up straight and tapped the paper. "Alright. Christmas Eve. We enter through the alley. Harold disables the alarm. Frank waits two blocks down with the van. Dot monitors the gala chatter and the Town Hall channel with her hearing aids and radio. We get in, get the cash, get out."

Dot raised her hand again. "What do we do with the money?"

"We deliver it anonymously the next morning," Edna said. "Drop donations at the food bank, the church, the shelter, and the community center. Wrapped, labeled, and clean. Let the people think it came from a miracle."

Harold tilted his head. "And if we're caught?"

Edna smiled. "We plead old age and good intentions."

Frank chuckled low in his throat. "That's actually not a bad plan."

"Then it's settled," Edna said, raising her mug of lukewarm tea. "One week from now, the Santa Squad saves Christmas."

They clinked mugs, four mismatched hands coming together in the soft light of the common room.

Outside, the wind blew gently against the windowpanes. Snow was falling again, covering the sidewalks and streets in white.

But inside Evergreen, the air was charged with something far stronger than the storm — a plan, a purpose, and a promise.

The town didn't know it yet, but help was coming.

And it was wearing orthopedic shoes.

Chapter 4

It was strange how quickly an ordinary week could turn into something extraordinary.

At Evergreen Retirement Home, the days had always blended together like oatmeal—soft, bland, and mostly beige. But now? There was a spark in the air. A fizz. A twinkle of something secret and exciting, tucked between crossword puzzles and pudding cups.

For the Santa Squad, the countdown to Christmas Eve had officially begun.

And it was time to train.

. . .

The first training session took place in the south hallway, just after lunch, when most residents were napping and the staff were switching shifts. It was the quietest stretch of corridor in the building—and conveniently lined with fake ficus plants and awkwardly placed coat racks that made excellent "obstacles."

Edna led the session with the seriousness of a general preparing for battle. She'd even brought a whistle. Where she got it, no one asked.

"Alright, team," she barked, hands on hips. "Today's lesson: Stealth 101."

Frank groaned. "I already regret everything."

"You always regret everything," Edna shot back. "Now, eyes forward. This isn't about speed. It's about silence, shadows, and slipping past nosy neighbors."

She held up a fuzzy red scarf. "This is the target. Someone has to steal it from the hallway coat hook without being seen by our 'security camera'—that's Dot."

Dot was perched on a folding chair down the hall, her knitting needles clicking away. She looked more like someone's grandmother waiting for a bus than a lookout, but her hearing aids were on full power, and her eyesight was sharper than anyone gave her credit for.

Harold went first. He crept along the wall in his slippers, trying his best to stay out of view. Unfortunately, his knee cracked with every step, and he let out a small yelp when he bumped his elbow on a coat rack.

"Busted!" Dot called sweetly.

"Drat," Harold muttered, rubbing his elbow.

Frank went next. His idea of stealth was walking at a normal pace and pretending he wasn't doing anything suspicious. Dot spotted him immediately.

"Too casual," Edna called. "You looked like you were about to rob the vending machine."

"I *was* about to rob the vending machine," Frank mumbled.

Dot giggled from her post.

Then came Edna's turn. She moved slowly, hunched low, using the ficus plants as cover. She paused behind a recycling bin, peeked around the corner, then inched forward.

Dot blinked, confused. "Where'd she go?"

"I don't believe it," Harold whispered. "She's actually good."

Edna snatched the red scarf, tucked it into her cardigan, and strutted back down the hall.

Dot clapped. "Amazing! You vanished like a Christmas ninja!"

Edna gave a satisfied grin. "Thank you. Years of sneaking up on my children when they were trying to steal cookies."

Frank muttered, "Should've been arrested years ago."

Later that afternoon, they met in the arts-and-crafts room to work on disguises. Dot brought a box of old costumes left over from a previous

Halloween event, while Harold brought two Santa hats and a pair of novelty glasses with a fake mustache attached.

Frank refused to wear anything with jingle bells.

"I'm not jingling my way through a crime scene," he said flatly.

Instead, they settled on festive scarves, oversized coats, and floppy hats—just enough to look like confused carolers or grandparents on a stroll, not four retirees with a mission.

They practiced their "roles" in the hallway, waving at the occasional nurse or fellow resident like nothing was out of the ordinary.

"Distraction is key," Edna said, adjusting her hat. "If anyone sees us, we smile, say 'Merry Christmas,' and keep moving."

Harold added, "Or we ask for directions to the bathroom. Works every time."

Dot pulled out a notepad she'd started keeping in her purse. "Should we come up with code names?"

Edna perked up. "Yes! Every team needs code names."

Frank rolled his eyes. "Please don't."

Dot ignored him. "I want to be Snowflake."

Harold smiled. "I'll be Frost."

"Gingerbread," Edna said proudly.

They all looked at Frank.

He crossed his arms. "No."

"Come on, Frank," Edna coaxed. "You need a name."

Frank sighed. "...Blizzard."

Dot squealed. "Ooh! That's perfect. Scary and wintery!"

"It fits your personality," Harold added with a smirk.

Frank grunted, but he didn't argue.

As the days went on, their "training" expanded. They practiced speaking into walkie-talkies in the garden shed, tested how fast Harold could open a locked filing cabinet (47 seconds), and even tried loading empty boxes into Frank's van behind the building without being seen.

Dot stood guard every time, her hearing aids tuned like radar.

"I haven't had this much fun since 1984," she said one evening as they sat together in the lounge.

Harold looked up from his tea. "Really?"

Dot nodded. "That was the year I and my husband took ballroom dancing lessons. We were awful. But it was exciting. Silly. And it felt like we were doing something just for us."

Edna looked over. "Do you miss him?"

Dot smiled gently. "Every day. But this?" She waved her hand at the group. "This makes me feel alive again. Needed."

Harold nodded slowly. "It's strange. I spent most of my life telling people to use quiet voices and keep their hands to themselves. But now? I'm sneaking around with radios in my socks."

Frank snorted. "You all talk like this is some grand adventure."

"It is," Edna said. "We've been pushed to the sidelines so long, we started believing we belonged there. But look at us now. Planning. Training. Working together."

She paused. "And we're doing it for others."

Frank didn't respond. But a moment later, he looked up and said, "I drove the van around the block today."

Everyone turned to him.

"It still runs," he said. "Brakes are a little soft. But she'll do."

Edna smiled. "Good. Because Christmas Eve is coming fast."

That night, as the residents of Evergreen turned off their lights and the halls went still, the Santa Squad sat together one last time before bed.

They weren't just four people with aches and pill organizers anymore.

The Christmas Heist

They were a team.

They were friends.

And for the first time in a long time... they had purpose.

Chapter 5

Two nights before Christmas Eve, the Santa Squad gathered in the parking lot behind Evergreen under a sky full of stars.

Edna glanced at her watch. "7:02. Good. Right on time."

Dot adjusted her scarf and looked around nervously. "Are we sure this is a good idea?"

"No," Frank said flatly. "That's why we're doing a practice run."

They were bundled in coats, gloves, and mismatched winter hats. Frank's van sat idling behind them, coughing out little puffs of exhaust. Harold stood nearby with a clipboard, his breath fogging in the cold air as he ticked off items on a checklist.

"Tonight is our dress rehearsal," Edna announced. "We go through every part of the plan. Timing, entry, exit. We treat it like the real thing — minus the actual breaking and entering."

Dot's eyes widened. "So... no safe cracking?"

"Not tonight," Harold said. "But we'll simulate the steps so we're ready for the real deal."

"Can we still wear our code names?" Dot asked.

Edna smiled. "Of course, Snowflake."

Dot beamed and tugged her hat down snug.

"Alright," Edna said. "Let's get in character."

They piled into the van — Dot and Harold in the back, Edna riding shotgun. Frank slid into the driver's seat, grumbling about cold steering wheels.

He pulled the van away from Evergreen with surprising smoothness, easing it out onto the quiet neighborhood road. The snow had stopped earlier that afternoon, but the streets were still blanketed in white, sparkling under the streetlamps.

As they drove through town, Dot looked out the window. "Look at the lights."

Every house seemed to glow with a warm, golden hue. Wreaths on doors. Twinkling trees in windows. Inflatable snowmen waved at passing cars. It was the kind of peaceful scene you might find on the front of a holiday card — and a sharp contrast to what they were planning.

Harold watched the streets carefully. "We'll take this route on the night of the job. Fewer stoplights. Less chance of traffic."

Frank nodded. "Good. The van doesn't like stopping too often."

Edna turned to look at him. "It's not the van I'm worried about. It's the driver."

"I've had a license longer than you've had gray hair."

"I started going gray at thirty," she shot back.

"Exactly."

Dot giggled in the back seat. "We're going to jail."

They arrived at their destination: the Evergreen Community Center.

It wasn't Town Hall, of course, but it was close enough in layout — similar building size, same double-door entrance, even a keypad alarm on the side entrance that Harold insisted was "purely decorative."

"This'll be our practice site," Edna said. "No one uses this wing after six."

"Alright," Harold said, hopping out of the van. "Let's move."

Frank parked under a large pine tree to simulate their actual drop-off point.

Edna and Harold took the lead, heading around to the side door.

Dot stayed inside the van with her walkie-talkie. She wore her headset and listened closely, the little green light blinking beside her ear.

"Radio check," Harold whispered into his mic.

"Loud and clear," Dot whispered back.

Harold grinned. "Good. Santa Squad is officially online."

Edna turned to him. "Ready to breach?"

"I was born ready."

The side door of the community center wasn't locked — thankfully — and they slipped inside, careful to close it gently behind them. The corridor was dark, quiet, and smelled faintly of lemon cleaner and dust.

Edna held a flashlight wrapped in red tissue paper to dull the beam.

"Proceeding to office area," she whispered into the walkie.

"Roger that, Gingerbread," came Dot's reply.

They moved slowly down the hallway, avoiding squeaky tiles and ducking past windows like overgrown children playing spies. At one point, Harold accidentally bumped into a janitor's cart and froze in place like a deer in headlights.

The Christmas Heist

"It's empty," Edna whispered. "Keep moving."

They reached a supply closet and used it to simulate Grafton's office.

"Time me," Harold said. He pulled out a small combination lock and crouched in front of it like a surgeon preparing for a delicate operation.

Frank's voice came through the walkie. "This is Blizzard. Still no signs of life outside. Over."

Edna pressed her mic. "Copy that. Operation Eggnog is in progress."

Harold snorted but didn't look up. "Who comes up with these names?"

"Me," Edna said proudly. "Now hush and open that lock."

Harold worked quickly, his fingers nimble for someone who once claimed he had arthritis in four knuckles. Within forty seconds, the lock popped open with a soft click.

"Boom," he whispered. "Safe cracked."

Edna gave him a slow clap. "Very impressive, Frost."

Dot's voice chirped in. "There's a couple walking their dog outside. Big coat. German shepherd."

"Noted," Edna said. "Let us know if they turn toward the building."

Dot replied, "Negative. They're walking past."

Harold stood and dusted off his knees. "Alright. Grab the loot."

They picked up two reams of printer paper to simulate the cash and stuffed them into a canvas tote. It was heavier than expected, but Harold just grinned.

"Cardio and crime. Who says we don't exercise?"

Edna smirked. "Let's move. Santa's got deliveries to make."

They retraced their steps, whispering updates into the walkie-talkies as they went. Dot kept a running tally of imaginary obstacles: "Snow plow approaching," "Christmas carolers down the block," "Possible raccoon by the dumpster."

Frank's voice crackled in every so often: "I think a parking meter just gave me a dirty look."

They reached the van, loaded the "loot," and slid back into their seats. Mission complete.

Back at Evergreen, they sat in the common room, cheeks flushed, hands wrapped around mugs of hot cocoa.

"That went surprisingly well," Harold said.

Dot nodded, still grinning. "I didn't lose radio contact once. And the walkie-talkies worked better than I expected."

"You were a good lookout," Edna told her. "Sharp as ever."

Dot's eyes misted. "I haven't felt useful in a long time. But tonight? I was part of something."

"You *are* something," Edna said gently. "We all are."

Frank took a long sip of cocoa. "I'll admit it. That was... actually kind of fun."

Edna raised her mug. "Then we're ready."

Harold raised his too. "Christmas Eve. One chance."

Frank added, "No mistakes."

Dot lifted hers last. "For the kids. For the coats. For the people who need it."

Their mugs clinked together in quiet celebration.

Outside, the stars twinkled overhead. The world looked peaceful. Calm.

But just beneath the surface, the Santa Squad was preparing to shake things up — not for mischief, but for a little holiday justice.

And for the first time in a long time, they felt like heroes.

Even if they had to sneak through the night in orthopedic shoes.

Chapter 6

Snow fell silently that night, blanketing the world outside Evergreen Retirement Home in white.

Inside, the building was hushed. Most residents had gone to bed early after a lively carol singalong in the main lounge. The decorations twinkled softly under dimmed lights—garlands wrapped around banisters, tiny wreaths hung on doors, and the tall Christmas tree in the corner stood proudly, its colored lights blinking like slow, thoughtful heartbeats.

It was quiet. But not empty.

In the reading room just off the main hallway, the Santa Squad sat together, not plotting or whispering into walkie-talkies this time, but resting. Reflecting. Waiting for something they couldn't quite name.

Edna sat by the fireplace, her feet tucked under her in a green plaid blanket, sipping tea from her favorite chipped mug. Dot curled in an armchair beside her, holding a half-finished scarf in her lap. Harold was on the sofa with a book he hadn't turned a page of in half an hour. Frank leaned against the windowsill, arms crossed, gazing out into the snowy night.

They had come here after their "final prep meeting," as Harold had called it—one last check of their plan, the radios, the disguise box. But the checklists were done, and now there was nothing left to do but wait for Christmas Eve.

And maybe remember.

It was Dot who broke the silence first.

"It always snows this week," she said softly, not looking up from her knitting. "Like the weather remembers even when we forget."

The Christmas Heist

Harold glanced over. "Forget what?"

"That feeling. When you're small and Christmas is still... magic." She smiled wistfully. "I still remember the Christmas I got my first bicycle. Red, with a white basket. I screamed so loud my dad nearly dropped his coffee."

Edna chuckled. "Did you ride it right away?"

"In the snow, yes. Slipped, fell, scraped my knee. Still worth it."

They lapsed into silence again. The fire crackled gently, sending flickers of light across the walls.

After a long pause, Frank spoke. "For me, it was 1979."

Everyone turned toward him. Frank wasn't usually the one to share.

He didn't move from the window, just stared out at the swirling snow.

"My wife, Millie, decorated everything that year. The tree, the porch, even the car dashboard. We had this little house just outside Cincinnati. Cold as anything. I was working two jobs back then—warehouse and night security—and I was always tired. Always too busy. But that Christmas?"

He paused. "I came home on Christmas Eve, and she'd waited up for me. The whole place was glowing. Cookies out, music playing. And she handed me this box wrapped in newspaper because she ran out of real paper. Inside was a watch. Just a little silver thing. Said she saved for months."

Frank cleared his throat. "She said, 'Now you'll know when it's time to come home.'"

Silence.

Then Dot wiped her eyes behind her glasses.

"What happened to her?" she asked gently.

"Cancer. '91. Quick." His voice was rough. "Too quick. I kept that watch until it stopped ticking. Still have it in my drawer."

No one said anything. They didn't need to.

After a moment, Edna said softly, "You must've loved her very much."

"I did." Frank turned from the window and sat down heavily in the chair by the bookcase. "Never remarried. Didn't seem worth trying to replace something that perfect."

Harold gave a slow, solemn nod. "I was married, too. Briefly. It didn't stick."

Edna raised an eyebrow. "What happened?"

"She liked jazz. I liked silence." He gave a small smile. "We didn't fight, just… faded out. Stayed friends. But holidays after that always felt a little quieter. Like the music stopped."

Dot reached over and patted his knee. "That's kind of sad."

"It's okay," Harold said. "I like quiet. It lets me remember the good parts."

They all nodded. The room felt full—not just of people, but of years, of echoes, of lives still unfolding in memories.

Edna took a deep breath, then set down her mug.

"I haven't talked to my daughter in six years," she said quietly.

The others looked at her in surprise. Edna, always the fearless one, the planner, the mouthy leader of their little gang, now sat with her shoulders curled inward.

"Her name's Michelle. She lives in Vermont. Runs a shop that sells handmade soaps and jam and all that wholesome stuff I never had the patience for."

She paused. "She and I... well, we're not alike. I was always working when she was young. Teaching, grading, running the house. Her dad—my husband—he was softer, easier. But he passed when she was in college. After that, it was just the two of us, and we didn't know how to talk to each other without him."

Dot leaned forward. "What happened six years ago?"

"She came to visit for Christmas. I'd just moved into Evergreen. I was still bitter. Angry at getting old, I suppose. She brought her two boys. I snapped at them. Told them to stop breaking things when they were just being kids." She sighed. "Michelle said, 'You always cared more about control than joy.' Then she left. I haven't heard from her since."

A heavy silence settled.

"She sends cards," Edna added, trying to smile. "The boys sign their names. But no phone calls. No visits. No pictures."

Dot's voice trembled. "Have you written her?"

Edna shook her head. "Too proud. Too scared."

Harold set down his book. "Maybe it's not too late."

"I don't know," Edna said. "Sometimes it feels like the train's already left the station."

Frank, surprisingly, spoke next. "You never know. Sometimes it circles back."

Dot wiped at her eyes again. "You should write to her, Edna. Or call. Just say Merry Christmas. It doesn't have to be perfect."

Edna looked at her hands. "I wouldn't even know what to say."

"Start with the truth," Harold said. "That you

miss her. That you wish you'd done it differently. That you're still here."

The fire popped loudly. Outside, the snow continued falling.

For a while, no one spoke. They just sat, sharing the silence like it was a warm quilt passed around the room.

Eventually, Edna stirred.

"You know, when I was a girl," she said, "we didn't get many presents. But my father used to leave a single orange in our stockings. One perfect orange. Said it was the rarest treasure he could find in winter."

Dot smiled. "Mine gave us walnuts. He said cracking them built character."

Harold chuckled. "My grandmother once gave me a potato painted gold. Said it was for 'wealth in the new year.' I believed her."

Even Frank laughed at that. "You were all conned by produce."

They burst into soft laughter, warm and real. It

rippled through the room, loosening the weight that had settled there minutes before.

Edna wiped her eye and looked toward the fire. "We've all lost something. But maybe that's why we're doing this. Not just to help others... but to remember we still can."

Harold nodded. "I think that's exactly why."

Dot leaned back in her chair and looked at the ceiling with a peaceful sigh. "I feel like I've come home in a strange way. Not to a place—but to people."

Frank didn't respond, but his face softened as he stared at the dancing flames.

They stayed there for another hour, sharing old stories, some funny, some sad. They spoke of siblings they hadn't seen in years, pets long gone, favorite dishes from Christmas past, songs that still made them cry.

They weren't just four old people anymore. They were friends. A patchwork family stitched together by timing, by choice, and by a cause bigger than themselves.

And beneath it all was the deep, unspoken truth: they were still living. Still learning. Still capable of love, loss, and laughter.

Even now.

Especially now.

When they finally stood to go back to their rooms, Dot hugged each of them.

"I know we're breaking into a government building tomorrow," she said softly, "but tonight? Tonight felt like Christmas already."

Edna smiled and touched her shoulder. "Thank you, Snowflake."

Harold gave a little salute. "Frost, signing off."

Frank shook his head. "Blizzard doesn't do hugs."

Dot hugged him anyway.

Later, in the quiet of her room, Edna pulled out a blank card from her desk drawer.

She sat at the edge of the bed, staring at the clean page, the pen heavy in her hand.

Then she began to write:

Dear Michelle,

I know it's been a long time. Too long. And I know I've made mistakes—more than I can list in a letter. But I'm thinking of you tonight. Of the boys. Of the Christmases we didn't get quite right. I want you to know I love you. I always have. I miss you. And if you'd like to talk... I'm still here.

Love,

Mom

She folded the letter carefully and slipped it into the envelope, unsure if she would ever send it.

But even writing it felt like a start.

Outside, the snow fell deeper. Tomorrow was Christmas Eve. The night of the heist.

But tonight? Tonight was about ghosts, yes—but also hope.

And maybe, just maybe, redemption.

Chapter 7

Christmas Eve arrived like a whispered promise—soft snow drifting from a pale gray sky, carolers bundled in scarves, and the scent of cinnamon and pine in every hallway of Evergreen Retirement Home.

The staff had hosted a cheerful holiday lunch. There were paper crowns from crackers, overcooked ham, and slightly lopsided cupcakes decorated by someone who clearly loved frosting more than balance. But for four specific residents, the day passed in a slow, thumping rhythm of anticipation.

It was time.

The Christmas Heist

Operation Christmas Heist was no longer a plan. It was happening.

By 6:30 p.m., the Santa Squad was assembled behind the maintenance shed.

They were dressed like Christmas exploded: oversized coats, scarves, hats with pom-poms, Harold's infamous sweater with flashing lights, and Dot's snowman earmuffs that looked like they were listening in on the mission themselves.

Frank's van waited by the back lot, engine quietly rumbling, heater running.

Dot adjusted her headset. "All radios working?"

"Check," came Harold's voice through the walkie-talkie.

"Check," echoed Edna.

Frank clicked his. "Still here. Still cold."

They each carried small packs—flashlights, gloves, tote bags, one thermos of coffee (Frank's), and, tucked in Harold's coat pocket, a set of improvised lockpicking tools that looked suspiciously like parts from a retired toaster.

"Alright," Edna whispered. "Let's move out. Step light, heads up. We're ghosts tonight."

Frank dropped them off two blocks from Town Hall at exactly 7:03 p.m.

The streets were mostly empty. Most of the town was either inside with family or gathered at the Mayor's Gala, which was already in full swing over at the Community Center. The soft sound of distant music echoed faintly through the snowy air.

The Town Hall stood tall and quiet under the streetlamp glow, a stately brick building with white columns and a wreath on every door. It looked serene. Innocent. But inside, according to Harold's recon, was a safe full of misappropriated donations.

"Ready, Frost?" Edna asked, her breath fogging the air.

Harold nodded and moved to the alley.

The Christmas Heist

They stopped by the utility box beside the staff door. Harold crouched and pulled off his gloves. His fingers worked with calm focus, tapping and prying.

Behind him, Edna stood watch. Dot's voice crackled softly in her ear.

"Crowd entering Gala now," she reported. "I saw Grafton himself. He's wearing a red bow tie and bragging about raffle tickets."

"Lovely," Edna replied. "He won't even notice we're gone."

Click.

The lock popped open. Harold grinned.

"Let's go."

Inside, Town Hall was still. No alarms. No beeping. Just the hum of old fluorescent lights and the faint ticking of a wall clock down the corridor.

"Alarm panel," Harold said, pointing.

He moved swiftly, unscrewed the cover, and tapped in a code—one he'd gleaned from a tech forum where someone posted default codes for the old model used here. Then he inserted a bent paperclip into the override slot.

Beep. Green light.

"No alarm," he whispered. "We're in the clear."

They crept down the hallway, past bulletin boards with faded announcements, a coat rack with one lonely umbrella, and a water fountain that coughed instead of bubbled.

Harold led them to the second floor.

"Remember," Edna said, "we're not here to make a mess. We're here to put things right."

They reached Grafton's office. Edna pulled out a hairpin. Harold raised an eyebrow.

"You planning to pick the lock too?"

"No," she said. "Just feel more confident with a weapon."

He chuckled and bent to the door. Within seconds, the knob gave way with a click.

They stepped into a room that smelled of paper and lemon polish. Heavy wooden furniture. Family photos on the desk. A shelf of dusty awards for "Civic Dedication." And on the wall—a large painting of a schooner.

Harold walked straight to it and lifted the frame.

"Bingo," he whispered.

Behind the painting was a small wall safe. Just as he'd remembered.

He knelt in front of it, opened his pouch, and pulled out tools.

"Time me."

Edna checked her watch. "You've got five minutes."

Outside, Dot's voice whispered again through the radio.

"All's calm. Grafton's at the dessert table. He just took three gingerbread men."

"Greedy," Edna murmured.

The tumblers in the safe clicked softly as Harold worked.

Edna looked around the office. She picked up a snow globe from Grafton's desk—a tiny replica of Town Hall itself, with fake snow swirling around miniature columns.

She shook it once, then set it down with a soft sigh.

"I used to think people like Grafton meant well," she said. "That maybe they just got tired. But this? This is selfish."

Harold nodded, eyes on the dial. "He had a choice."

Edna looked down. "We all do."

Click.

The safe opened.

Harold sat back and wiped his forehead.

Inside were neat bundles of cash, envelopes labeled with names like *Food Bank – December Disbursement*, *Winter Coat Drive*, and *Church Pantry Fund*.

It was all there.

Edna stared at it.

"It's more than I expected," she said quietly.

Harold began stuffing the bundles into their tote bags, careful not to disturb the order.

Dot's voice came in again, quieter now.

"Uh... small problem. Tyler the security guy just stepped out of the Gala. He's walking toward Town Hall."

Edna froze. "How far?"

"Just left the parking lot. He's got a thermos and a sandwich. Looks like he's doing his round early."

"Stall him if you can," Edna said. "Frank, do you copy?"

Frank's voice crackled back. "Blizzard here. I'm three minutes away. Warming the engine."

Harold zipped the last bag.

"Let's move."

They crept back out of the office, down the hall, and back toward the stairwell. Their bags were heavy, but they didn't slow down.

Dot's voice came again. "Tyler's at the corner. If he rounds it, he'll see the side door open."

"Tell us when he's fifteen seconds away," Edna said.

The stairwell door squeaked when Harold pushed it open.

"Hold it," Edna whispered. She pulled out a small tin of petroleum jelly from her coat pocket and dabbed it along the hinges.

Harold blinked. "You thought of everything."

"I used to live with a teenage boy. Nothing squeaks if you want to catch them sneaking out."

They made it down the stairs in record time. Harold resealed the alarm panel. Edna pushed the door closed.

"Tyler's halfway across the lot," Dot said, urgency in her voice.

"Now," Edna whispered.

The Christmas Heist

They darted around the side of the building, boots crunching lightly on the snow, just as Frank's van pulled around the corner, headlights off, moving like a ghost.

He popped the back door.

"In!" he barked.

They threw themselves into the van. Harold slammed the door shut.

Frank didn't wait for instructions. He drove.

Behind them, Tyler stood in the snow, sipping his thermos, blissfully unaware.

They didn't speak until they were two blocks away.

Then Edna let out a long breath.

"Well," she said. "We just robbed a government building."

Harold looked over. "Correction: We just *reclaimed stolen property*."

Dot's voice came through, giddy. "That was the most exciting thing I've done since disco!"

Even Frank allowed himself a grin. "We did it."

They drove in silence for a few moments, the quiet wrapping around them like a blanket.

Then Dot spoke again.

"Where do we take it?"

Edna turned in her seat to face the back. "We split it. Four stops. One each. Tonight. Quiet and clean."

"I'll take the church pantry," Harold said.

"Food bank," Frank added.

"I'll handle the community center," Edna said. "They open at dawn."

"I'll do the shelter," Dot said softly. "It's on the same street as my niece's house. I'll make it look like an anonymous delivery."

"Perfect," Edna said. "Then tomorrow, the town wakes up to a Christmas miracle."

Harold smiled. "And no one knows the truth."

Edna looked out the window at the snow-covered houses.

"They don't need to," she said. "The point is, the right people get what they need. That's what Christmas should be."

Frank's van turned back onto the quiet road leading to Evergreen.

No lights. No sirens. Just the hush of snow and the hum of purpose.

Their work wasn't done—but the hardest part was.

And as they approached the soft glow of home, Dot said it best:

"We're not just the Santa Squad anymore."

"Oh?" Harold asked. "Then who are we?"

She smiled. "We're the ghosts of Christmas *present*."

And somewhere in the stillness of the snowy night, they all felt it—

That this year, they hadn't just saved Christmas.

They'd brought it back to life.

Chapter 8

The snow was still falling gently as Frank's van rumbled back into the Evergreen parking lot just before 9:00 p.m. The mission had gone off without a hitch. The Santa Squad had successfully entered Town Hall, reclaimed the misused Christmas funds, and divvied up the deliveries for their final round of midnight miracles.

Now, each member had one stop left before the town awoke to find that Christmas had quietly, humbly, and completely returned to the people it belonged to.

The Christmas Heist

Dot had volunteered to go last. She sat in the passenger seat now with a labeled envelope in her lap: *Hope Street Shelter.* Inside it was just over $1,100 in carefully rubber-banded bills. Enough for food, warm bedding, and new coats for families who'd otherwise have had little more than cold floors and colder meals.

"You sure you want to do this alone?" Edna asked, tugging her scarf a little tighter. "I can ride with you."

Dot smiled gently. "It's on the way to my niece's house. I told her I might stop by to leave cookies on the porch. She'll never know the difference."

Edna gave her a long look, then nodded. "You've got this, Snowflake."

"Roger that, Gingerbread," Dot whispered, giving her a little salute.

Harold passed her a paper bag. "Put the envelope inside. Tie the bag. Leave it by the door. In and out."

Dot took it and tucked it safely inside her oversized tote.

Frank rolled down the driver's side window and muttered, "If anyone gets caught tonight, it's going to be because you all keep using codenames like it's World War II."

"You love it," Edna shot back with a grin.

Frank didn't deny it.

He dropped Dot off at the corner of Hope Street just before 9:30. The shelter was dark, save for a single light glowing above the side entrance. Dot could see a few silhouettes moving inside—volunteers tidying up after dinner, probably. She waited until Frank had pulled away and the coast was clear.

Then she stepped into the snow.

It was quiet. Peaceful.

She crossed the short path to the door, her heart fluttering in her chest. Not from fear—but from something else. Something that felt like… purpose.

She placed the bag gently against the door and stepped back.

The Christmas Heist

Just as she turned to leave, a voice cut through the silence.

"Excuse me—ma'am?"

Dot froze.

Behind her, the door had opened. A young man in a volunteer jacket stood in the doorway, frowning in confusion.

"Were you dropping something off?"

Dot spun around with what she hoped was a kindly, innocent expression. "Oh! Hello. Yes. Just... some cookies. From my church group. We wanted to spread a little joy."

The man blinked. "At 9:30 p.m.?"

Dot hesitated. "It's a very committed church."

He looked down at the bag. "This isn't cookies."

Dot swallowed. "Oh dear. Did I leave the wrong bag?"

Before he could answer, another figure stepped out from behind him.

And Dot's heart stopped.

It was Tyler—the security guard from Town Hall.

The same Tyler who'd been at the Mayor's Gala. The same Tyler who had, just two hours earlier, taken a coffee break outside Town Hall, steps away from their heist.

"Oh no," Dot whispered.

Tyler squinted at her. "Wait a minute. I've seen you before."

"I—I don't think so," Dot stammered.

"Yeah," he said, stepping forward. "You're the lady from Evergreen. You're usually with that group—"

Dot straightened, lifted her chin, and said, very firmly, "Young man, I have no idea what you're talking about. But if you're implying I don't have the right to deliver baked goods to the needy on Christmas Eve, then I'd like to speak to your supervisor."

Tyler's mouth opened, then closed again.

Behind him, the volunteer looked between them, clearly confused.

"I mean," Tyler said, scratching his head, "if you're just making donations, that's fine, I guess..."

Dot smiled sweetly, stepping forward and patting the young man's shoulder.

"That's all it is, dear. A humble Christmas gift from a few old folks with big hearts and not much else."

Tyler looked down at the bag, then back at her.

She met his gaze.

After a long pause, he stepped aside.

"Well... Merry Christmas then," he mumbled.

Dot nodded politely. "And to you."

Then she turned, walked to the end of the street with dignity in every step, and didn't exhale until she saw Frank's van pull around the corner.

"Blimey," Frank muttered as Dot slid back into the front seat. "You alright?"

"I think I almost gave myself a stroke," Dot said, clutching her tote.

Edna's voice crackled through the walkie. "Snowflake, report."

"Gingerbread, I was nearly toasted."

Dot filled them in on the encounter as Frank drove.

Back at Evergreen, Edna and Harold stood outside the rear entrance waiting for them.

Harold held a blanket and a thermos. "For shock," he said seriously.

Dot took the blanket gratefully.

Frank shut off the engine. "That security guard—Tyler—he's getting too close for comfort."

Edna frowned. "We need to wrap this up, now."

"Then let's do it," Harold said.

Together, they climbed the back stairs to the second-floor lounge, where they'd agreed to debrief before morning. Once inside, Edna locked the door.

The Christmas Heist

Harold pulled out a battered folder and started making notes. "Donations delivered. All four locations. Anonymous, sealed. Everything accounted for."

"Except the brush with exposure," Dot said, sinking into her chair.

"You handled it," Edna said, placing a hand on her shoulder. "Like a pro."

Dot beamed, though her hands still trembled.

Then—just as Harold started to close the folder—a sharp knock echoed at the lounge door.

They all froze.

Another knock.

Frank stepped forward and peered through the small window.

"Uh-oh."

He opened the door just a crack.

And there stood **Mr. Grafton**.

His wool coat was dusted with snow, and his bow tie was slightly askew. His cheeks were red, but his eyes were cold.

"I need to speak with you," he said.

Frank blinked. "All of us?"

"Yes. I believe you know what this is about."

Frank didn't answer, but stepped aside.

Grafton entered the lounge and looked around at the four of them. His hands were stuffed in his pockets. His expression was hard to read—equal parts suspicion and confusion.

"You four were seen near Town Hall tonight," he began. "By a city worker. He says you were carrying bags."

Edna stepped forward, cool and calm.

"We took a walk," she said. "It's Christmas Eve. Sometimes people take walks."

"At eight o'clock?"

"It's not illegal."

Harold chimed in. "I needed air. My doctor recommends it."

Grafton narrowed his eyes. "You expect me to believe that's all it was?"

The Christmas Heist

"Yes," Edna said simply.

There was a long pause.

Then, Grafton pulled something from his coat pocket.

A photograph.

He laid it on the table.

It showed Dot, just outside the shelter, talking to Tyler. The lighting was poor, but her profile was unmistakable.

Dot's face went pale.

"You want to explain this?" Grafton asked.

Dot opened her mouth—but nothing came out.

Then Edna leaned forward.

"That's not Dot," she said.

Grafton blinked. "Excuse me?"

"That's Mrs. Thomas. From the second floor. We gave her our Christmas cookies to deliver to the shelter. She's very generous. And has an unfortunate resemblance to Dot when viewed from a poor angle."

Grafton scoffed. "And what about the bags? The envelopes? The anonymous donations that just *happened* to appear at four separate charities tonight?"

"Sounds like a miracle," Harold said dryly.

Frank shrugged. "Tis the season."

Grafton's nostrils flared.

"You think this is funny?"

"No," Edna said. "We think it's done."

He stepped back, clearly frustrated.

"If I find out you've tampered with town property—"

"You'll do what?" Edna said calmly. "Arrest four senior citizens? Try us in the court of public opinion? Accuse us of… what exactly? Delivering anonymous holiday donations?"

Grafton stared at her. But she didn't flinch.

Then, slowly, he tucked the photo back in his coat pocket.

"You're not clever," he said through gritted teeth.

"No," Edna replied, "we're just tired of watching greedy men ruin good things."

And with that, Grafton turned on his heel and left.

The door clicked shut behind him.

There was silence for a moment.

Then Harold let out a breath. "That was close."

Dot nodded shakily. "I thought I was done for."

Edna picked up the photo he left behind and tucked it into the fireplace, watching the edges curl and blacken.

"We're not done," she said softly. "Not yet. But we're safe. And more importantly…"

She turned to them all.

"We did it."

Chapter 9

Christmas morning arrived the way it always did — quietly, gently, as if not to wake the world too fast. A soft hush hung over Evergreen Retirement Home, broken only by the occasional creak of footsteps and the distant jingling of a music box playing "Silent Night."

But this year… something was different.

It started with a knock at the community center's side door just before dawn.

Linda, the part-time janitor and unofficial town gossip, had come in early to make coffee for the breakfast crew. When she opened the door, she found a bag on the doorstep — neatly packed, labeled, and sealed.

Inside: a fat envelope of cash, some handwritten notes that read *"For the children's holiday meal fund,"* and a second envelope stuffed with local gift cards.

At 7:15 a.m., a volunteer at the Hope Street Shelter came out to shovel the steps and found a box wrapped in brown paper sitting under the mail slot. Inside were dozens of crisp bills bundled with notes that read *"For warm bedding, coats, and food."*

At 7:40, the town church pantry received its own miracle — a sealed bag left outside the donation shed, packed with exactly enough to cover the pantry's winter deficit and then some.

And by 8:05, word had already begun to spread.

By 8:30, the town was buzzing.

Inside Evergreen's dining hall, the Santa Squad sat together at their usual table, bundled in festive sweaters, sipping cocoa and acting —

quite convincingly — like they knew nothing about the sudden generosity sweeping through Mapleton.

Dot stirred her cocoa with both hands wrapped around the mug, her eyes sparkling as she listened to the excited chatter from nearby tables.

"I heard someone left over two grand at the food bank!" said Mrs. Chandler, who hadn't heard anything that clearly in years but somehow always knew everything before it hit the paper.

"No name, no note," whispered Mr. Kline. "Just said 'Merry Christmas.' Can you imagine?"

Dot smiled. "Sounds like a Christmas angel."

Harold, seated beside her, looked particularly pleased with himself. His tie was crooked, and his eyes were bright behind his glasses.

Frank muttered, "All we need now is a skywriter."

Edna sipped her tea, one eyebrow raised. "No need. The town's doing all the writing for us."

The Christmas Heist

Sure enough, the morning news broadcast on the old television mounted above the fireplace flicked to a breaking update.

"—community still buzzing this Christmas morning after multiple charities reported anonymous donations overnight. Volunteers are calling it a 'Christmas miracle' and say the timing couldn't have been better."

The reporter was standing outside the community center, her cheeks red from the cold, smiling into the camera.

"Officials have no leads on who left the packages, though one note found tucked into a coat delivery simply read, *'From someone who remembers what Christmas is for.'*"

Dot's hand flew to her heart.

Edna turned to her with a small smile. "Yours?"

Dot nodded shyly. "I just... I wanted them to know someone cared."

Harold leaned forward. "You know, I've read about towns where people leave 'miracle money' every year. Always anonymous. But you can feel it ripple through everything. It's not just about the cash — it's about hope."

Frank grunted. "Well, I hope no one decides to return the favor and investigate the surveillance footage."

Edna waved a hand. "Let them. We wore scarves. And Harold looked like a disco ball in that sweater."

"Camouflage," Harold said proudly.

Across the room, Margaret, the activities director, stood and clapped her hands for attention.

"Good morning, everyone! Merry Christmas! We have some special deliveries this morning from local families — a few of our residents have received packages!"

The residents perked up like schoolchildren.

Margaret called out a few names — a fruit basket for Mrs. Patel, a stack of books for Mr. Crane — then turned to Edna's table.

"And Edna Bishop — this one's for you."

Edna blinked.

The Christmas Heist

Margaret carried over a large envelope, decorated with candy cane stickers and a child's scrawled handwriting: *To Grandma Edna — from Logan & Sam!*

Dot gasped. "Your grandkids?"

Edna took the envelope with trembling hands. Inside was a folded card with glitter-glued snowmen on the front.

Dear Grandma Edna,

Mommy said I could write to you. We miss you. Can we come visit soon? I got a sled! Logan got a truck. Merry Christmas!

Love, Sam & Logan

Tucked inside was another, neater note in an adult's handwriting.

Mom,

The boys asked about you. I thought maybe it was time.

I hope you're doing okay.

Merry Christmas.

—Michelle

Edna sat silently for a moment.

Then slowly, carefully, she folded the note and placed it in her lap. Her hands trembled as she wiped at her eyes.

"I guess the train does come back," she whispered.

Dot leaned over and squeezed her hand. "I'm so glad you wrote her."

Harold smiled. "Sometimes all it takes is a little courage. And a good postal system."

Frank pretended to wipe something from his eye and muttered, "Allergies."

Later that morning, the four of them slipped away to the second-floor lounge, mugs in hand, a plate of shortbread cookies between them.

They sat in comfortable silence, the kind shared only by people who had done something quietly extraordinary together.

Edna looked out the window at the snowy town below.

"Do you think they'll ever know?" she asked.

"I hope not," Harold replied. "Miracles work best when no one's looking."

Dot giggled. "Well, we were definitely not built for subtlety."

Frank reached for a cookie. "We're retired. We've earned the right to break a few rules."

Edna nodded slowly. "Still... I think this was more than just one good deed. I think we reminded ourselves of something."

"That we're still useful," Dot said quietly.

"That we still matter," Harold added.

Frank nodded. "That we're still alive."

They all looked at one another.

And in that small, sunlit lounge with the heater humming and the windows fogging from the warmth of cocoa and friendship, they didn't feel old. Or forgotten. Or on the sidelines.

They felt full. Present. Seen.

And just as Edna opened her mouth to speak, Margaret's voice echoed through the intercom.

"Attention residents: this afternoon at three o'clock, we'll be holding a special screening of *It's a Wonderful Life* in the activity room. Cookies and hot cider provided. Bring your holiday spirit!"

Harold groaned. "They play that movie every year."

Dot beamed. "And every year, I cry."

Frank rolled his eyes. "You cried during *Die Hard* last week."

"Bruce Willis was very brave," she insisted.

Edna chuckled. "I say we go. We've earned it."

They all stood, slowly, with the measured grace of people whose knees didn't quite cooperate anymore.

Frank stretched. "Next year, maybe we'll take a break from crime."

Dot smiled. "Next year, maybe we just bake cookies."

"Or mail money to people the old-fashioned way," Harold said.

The Christmas Heist

Edna paused at the door.

"Maybe. But if the world ever forgets what Christmas is for again…"

She turned, that old sparkle in her eye.

"We'll remind it."

They nodded in agreement.

And somewhere beneath the snow-covered streets of Mapleton, the spirit of Christmas pulsed a little brighter — thanks to four unlikely heroes who'd dared to believe they still had something to give.

Chapter 10

The sun peeked over the snowy rooftops of Mapleton, casting long golden beams across the quiet town.

Inside Evergreen Retirement Home, the halls hummed with quiet cheer. Wreaths hung from every door, cinnamon rolls were baking in the kitchen, and Bing Crosby crooned softly from the lobby speakers. Residents moved a little slower than usual, but their smiles were brighter. Something had changed — something they couldn't quite name.

And somewhere, deep down, they all felt it:

Christmas had come back. The real kind.

The Christmas Heist

. . .

Edna stepped into the dining hall wearing her red cardigan with the holly buttons and a sparkle in her eyes that rivaled the tree in the corner.

She spotted her usual table—and paused.

Dot was already seated, sipping cocoa and humming "O Come All Ye Faithful" softly under her breath.

Harold sat beside her, flipping through the morning paper with an almost smug little smile. "Miracle Donations Sweep Through Mapleton," the headline read. Below it, a photo of the community center with a giant red bow.

And Frank—grumpy, reliable Frank—sat across from them, already buttering a biscuit like it had personally offended him.

Edna pulled out a chair. "Merry Christmas, mischief-makers."

They all murmured their greetings, clinking mugs together in celebration.

Dot smiled shyly. "I got a message this morning. From my niece. She said she saw my name on the shelter's delivery note. Wants to know if I'd like to come to dinner next week."

"You going?" Frank asked.

"I am," Dot said. "I even bought a new sweater. It has jingle bells on the collar."

Frank made a face. "Of course it does."

Harold folded his newspaper and set it aside. "I've decided to teach a mystery writing workshop in the new year."

Edna raised an eyebrow. "Since when?"

"Since last night," he said. "Seems the world could use a few more clever plots and satisfying endings."

Frank snorted. "Just don't model the villains after me."

"No promises."

"And you?" Harold asked, turning to Edna.

She reached into her coat pocket and pulled

out a small, crumpled envelope. "My daughter called."

Everyone froze.

"She and the boys are driving up next week. We're going to bake cookies and watch old movies. She said she wants to… start over."

Dot clapped her hands. "Edna, that's wonderful!"

Frank nodded once. "Told you. Train always comes back."

"I never thought it would," Edna said softly. "But I guess… sometimes you just have to make the first move."

Harold smiled. "Seems like we all did, this year."

They sat for a moment in silence, letting the weight of that settle.

Then Edna raised her mug. "To the Santa Squad."

Dot lifted hers. "To purpose."

Harold joined in. "To second chances."

Frank raised his last. "To a clean getaway."

They clinked mugs, the sound light and cheerful, like sleigh bells in a far-off field.

Later that morning, the common room filled with laughter and music. Residents opened small gifts from family. Volunteers passed out warm pastries and cider. Someone played piano — badly, but no one seemed to mind.

And in the corner of the room, the Santa Squad watched it all from their seats near the fire.

They didn't need credit. Or thanks.

It was enough to see it all happening — joy, connection, hope.

This was what they'd fought for. What they'd broken a few rules for. What they'd reminded themselves and their town:

That Christmas wasn't about presents or perfect trees.

It was about showing up. Giving back. Making things right, even when the world didn't expect you to.

Especially then.

As the room filled with singing and the scent of peppermint, Margaret the activities director approached with a clipboard and her ever-bubbly grin.

"Alright, team," she said. "We've got Christmas karaoke starting in ten minutes. I need volunteers. Who's ready to belt out *Jingle Bell Rock*?"

Harold shook his head. "Absolutely not."

Dot perked up. "I'll do it if Edna joins me."

Edna laughed. "I'll sing only if Frank dances."

Frank scowled. "You want this to be a joyful event, not a medical emergency."

But ten minutes later, somehow, there they all were.

Dot and Edna up at the mic, singing off-key but full of heart. Harold tapping his foot along, harmonizing under his breath. And Frank — dear, stubborn Frank — doing a slow shuffle that might have been a dance, or just a very committed attempt to not fall over.

People clapped. Laughed. Even cheered.

And in that moment, surrounded by joy, Edna looked at her friends and thought:

This is the real miracle.

Not just what they'd done.

But who they'd become.

That night, as the snow fell again outside the windows and the lights dimmed to a golden glow, Edna sat in her room and pulled out the envelope from Michelle one more time.

She re-read the boys' drawing — a crooked snowman and a heart with "Grandma" written inside it.

And she smiled.

Then she picked up her pen and began writing a new card.

Dear Michelle,

The Christmas Heist

I can't wait to see you. Bring the sled. Bring the boys. And bring stories. I've got plenty of cocoa and maybe more cookies than we can eat. Let's start fresh. Let's start now.

At the same time, Dot slipped her new jingle-bell sweater over her head and laid out the gift her niece had sent — a small framed photo of them from a family picnic years ago. She placed it beside her bedside lamp and smiled.

Harold, back in his room, opened a blank notebook and titled the first page: *The Santa Squad: A Holiday Caper.*

Then, underneath: *Based on a Mostly True Story.*

And Frank?

He stood by his window, hands in his robe pockets, watching the snow.

He didn't say much.

But for once, he didn't need to.

Because Frank — tough, grumpy, guarded Frank — was smiling.

. . .

the end